GHOST TRAIN TO NOWHERE

Phil Roxbee Cox

Illustrated by
Jane Gedye

Series Editor: Gaby Waters

Contents

Reader Beware . . .

This is a chilling ghost story - but there's more to it than meets the eye. The mystery will unravel as the story unfolds, but if you keep your eyes open you may be able to solve it yourself.

Vital information might be lurking anywhere. On almost every double page there are things that could help you. The pictures are important, so look at them carefully. And make sure you read the old documents thoroughly. But don't be fooled. There may be some false clues . . .

Page 48 will give you some hints of what to look out for. You can refer to this page as you go along or look at it at the end to see if you missed anything.

The Arrival

When twins Alf and Chrissy first saw their Uncle Jack's house, they were in for a surprise. "You live in a station!" gasped Chrissy.

"It used to be a station," nodded Uncle Jack, lifting their luggage out of his car. "But a train hasn't stopped in Seabry for over eighty years." The twins picked up their backpacks and followed their uncle onto the old station platform. Chrissy was sure she heard the distant hoot of an owl.

That's odd, she thought. Owls are night birds. Even though it was a blazing hot summer's day, a cold shiver ran down her spine. Suddenly, the leaves on the trees in the nearby wood began to rustle, but there was no wind. In fact, there was an odd stillness in the air.

Both twins were overcome by a strange feeling. It was a feeling of excitement and anxiety and of mysterious things to come . . .

The Broken Pane

Passing through the front door, the twins immediately sensed that they were being watched. A pair of unblinking eyes stared at them through a small window in the wall to their right.

Meow.

"Meet Salmon," said Uncle Jack. "He's one in a long line of cats who has lived in this station. Station cats used to be paid an official wage to catch rats and mice."

They were standing in a large room crammed full of furniture. The twins looked around in interest.

"This used to be the waiting room," Uncle Jack explained.

"So that must have been the old ticket office," said Alf, walking over to where Salmon was sitting, watching them closely. The twins explored their new surroundings. Every picture, every ornament and every book had something to do with trains.

This place is like a museum.

A museum with a secret.

"Where are we going to sleep?" Alf asked. Uncle Jack pointed to a door marked 'LEFT LUGGAGE OFFICE'. Chrissy could feel Salmon's big green eyes following her as she walked over to it. She shivered again. Why did such a bright and cheerful house make her feel so strangely cold? It didn't make sense.

In their bedroom they found shelves of dusty trunks and suitcases left by passengers long ago, never to be reclaimed. Uncle Jack left the twins to unpack their own things, and went to boil some eggs.

Alf stuffed all his clothes into one drawer, then went over to the window. He looked out at the wooded valley sloping into the distance and wondered where the trains used to go once they left the station.

"The old track might still be out there," he said, then leaped back in surprise.

Without the slightest sound, a crack was slowly forming in the glass. It was zig-zagging its way up the middle of the window, only inches from Alf's face.

Chrissy looked on in utter amazement.

Something in the Woods

Uncle Jack claimed he wasn't bothered by the broken window. "It was probably the heat," he said. "The sun has been shining on it all day. Sometimes, if it gets too hot, glass cracks like that . . . especially glass around here." Alf and Chrissy were unconvinced by his explanation. He was studying them with a strange look in his eyes. Then again, it could just have been a trick of the light.

That night, Alf lay in bed staring up at the ceiling. Silvery moonlight shone through the window and the flimsy curtain, projecting the crack onto the ceiling as a jagged black line. He couldn't take his eyes off it.

Then something made him climb out of bed and pull back the curtain. It wasn't a voice in his head, but a sudden *need* to look out into the night. Chrissy opened a bleary eye. "Close the curtain will you? Some of us are trying to sleep," she groaned, lifting the bedclothes over her head.

As Alf was pulling the curtain back across the window, he caught sight of a puff of smoke coming from the woods.

"Chrissy!" he said in a harsh whisper. "Wake up."

"I wasn't asleep," said his sister. She joined him at the window and saw the smoke. "What's the big deal?" she asked. "Perhaps someone is camping out there in the woods and . . ." She stopped and pulled the curtain urgently across the window.

"What's the matter with you?" Alf asked.

"I've felt weird since we arrived, and now I've got the feeling that we're being watched," said Chrissy. "And what about that owl hoot in broad daylight?" She made a hooting noise by blowing air through her cupped hands.

TOOT!

"There *is* something freaky about this place," Alf admitted. He looked at the shadowy shapes of the long-forgotten luggage on the shelves. "Maybe it's having all this old stuff around us. It's exciting but creepy at the same time."

Alf couldn't get the image of the crack out of his mind. Glass didn't crack like that, so slowly and so silently. He felt the hairs on the back of his neck begin to rise . . . Now he too had a strong sense of being watched. He peered around the edge of the curtain into the silvery moonlight. Above the trees, the smoke had drifted away to nothing in the night air.

"I think we should investigate the smoke in the morning," said Chrissy. Something buried deep in her mind told her that the reason for their uneasiness lay out there in the woods. They would have to find out what it was if they didn't want any more sleepless nights.

Meanwhile, unknown to the twins, a shadowy figure lurked at the edge of the woods, avoiding the light of the moon. He stood in silence, watching and waiting, but waiting for what? And why?

The Stranger

The next morning, the twins had breakfast with Uncle Jack in the tiny kitchen that used to be the ticket office. Then they set off to explore the woods.

I've boiled you some eggs.

They walked through the trees until they reached a clearing at the bottom of a steep bank. "It's an old path," said Chrissy.

"Not a path," said Alf excitedly. "This must be where the old track used to be. Steam trains used to run along here."

"I wonder why they closed down the track?" Chrissy thought out loud.

"That's a very good question," said a voice. It was a dry, rasping voice. The voice of a stranger. The twins spun around. The voice belonged to an old man clutching a walking stick.

"You shouldn't have sneaked up on us like that," gulped Chrissy.

The stranger smiled. "I'm sorry," he said. "I took the easy route. You could have followed this old track straight from your uncle's house."

Chrissy felt that there was something odd about the old man. "How do you know who we are?" she asked suspiciously. "You just said our *uncle's* house."

I didn't mean to alarm you.

The stranger smiled. "There's no mystery in that," he said. "Seabry is a small village where everybody knows everybody else. My name is Harold Masters. I'm a very good friend of your uncle's. He told me that his twin nephew and niece were coming to stay. In fact, I've been looking forward to meeting you very much."

Chrissy felt stupid for not having trusted Harold Masters. Of course Uncle Jack would have told his friends that they were coming. She asked the old man if he had seen any smoke in the woods. The change that came over him was incredible. His eyes lit up with excitement and he pressed his face right up against hers. "You've seen smoke?" he asked urgently, as if it was the most important question in the world.

"Yes. Last night," said Alf. "From our bedroom window."

At that moment, there was an enormous clap of thunder, like some massive explosion, and a bolt of forked lightning seemed to split the clear blue sky in two. The blinding flash of light struck the branch of a tall tree to their left, setting it alight and ripping it from the trunk.

The blackened burning branch hurtled down toward them, flames streaking out like a comet's tail. "Look out!" screamed Alf.

The Thurhorn Bridge Disaster

It was a lucky escape. The huge branch only narrowly missed them. Chrissy felt the heat of the flames as it passed her face. There was a stunned silence, then Alf quickly helped Harold Masters to his feet. The old man had tripped in the scramble to save himself. Chrissy handed him his walking stick. The twins were shaking.

Thank you. I'm fine. I'm tougher than I look.

"If that had hit us . . ." began Alf.

"There's no point dwelling upon it," said Mister Masters. He seemed less surprised than the twins that a bolt of lightning should suddenly flash out of a clear blue sky. He ignored the blackened branch that still smouldered at their feet.

Chrissy turned and looked around her. There was an absolute stillness in the woods and no birds sang. "There's something strange about this place," she said. "It's quiet . . . too quiet . . . Something's *wrong*."

The twins could feel the old man's piercing eyes studying them intently. He cleared his throat. "Perhaps you could help put things right," he rasped.

"What do you mean?" asked Alf. The forked lightning had reminded him of the shape of the crack that had appeared in the window.

Harold Masters paused for a while before answering. It was as though he was trying to decide whether to share a secret with them or not. "I only know so much, and no more," he sighed. Chrissy noticed the old man had tears in his eyes.

"Does it have anything to do with the old track?" she asked. She didn't know what had made her ask that, or where the question even came from. The words just tumbled out of her mouth without her thinking.

Harold Masters nodded. "It has *everything* to do with the old track," he said, and told them a tragic tale . . .

When I was a boy, there were trains running up and down this track all the time. It was a very busy line.

All aboard!

Everyone in the village was proud of its station and the line that ran to Thurhorn.

Running like clockwork as usual.

Then, one winter's evening, disaster struck. My twin brother caught the 7:15 train from Seabry to Thurhorn. A terrible storm had been raging all day.

'Bye Harry.

'Bye Bill.

What nobody knew was that part of the bridge between here and Thurhorn had been washed away when the river burst its banks.

The train never reached Thurhorn. Nobody knows exactly what happened next, but an official inquiry said that it must have driven full speed off the end of the bridge. I never saw my brother again.

A Discovery

Neither Chrissy nor Alf knew what to say when the old man had finished his sorry story. He stood up and stared into the distance. "The bridge is some miles in that direction." He pointed. "This wood is so overgrown in parts that you'd get lost trying to follow the old track."

"Were there any survivors?" asked Alf, imagining the train plummeting to its watery grave.

"We never even found the train," said Harold Masters. "When it didn't arrive in Thurhorn, a search party from Seabry went out in the storm and found part of the bridge destroyed."

"The next day, the search party dragged the river and I was there, watching from the bank. They found nothing. The train and everyone on it was thought to have been washed out to sea by the raging torrent of the swollen river. The company closed the line soon after that. Since then, no earthly train has passed this way."

"*Earthly* train?" said Alf, mystified. "What do you mean? It's very sad Mister Masters, but what does it have to do with what's happening now?"

The old man frowned and studied the twins' faces before he spoke. "Perhaps things are about to change. Perhaps you can help. Nobody has ever believed me you see, but maybe you will . . . and things may start happening around here." With that, he walked away. "Come to my house tomorrow," he called over his shoulder. "Your uncle knows where I live."

Before Harold Masters was even out of sight, Alf turned to Chrissy and said: "We must follow the old track. Don't ask me why, I just *feel* we must." Chrissy didn't argue. She felt it too.

The farther they went, the more overgrown and difficult it was for the twins to follow the route of the old track. By late afternoon, there was no sign of where the track used to run, so they could only guess which way to go. By early evening, they were well and truly lost.

"We should have turned back when we still had a track to follow," sighed Chrissy. Her feet were aching from all the walking. She began to suspect that they'd been going around in circles. Then it started to rain.

"Brilliant," said Alf. "That's all we need."

Chrissy spotted what looked like a large cave in the hillside up ahead. "We can shelter in there," she said. As they got nearer, the twins realized that the cave wasn't a cave at all. It had brickwork around the edges. Alf broke into a run, dashing past his sister in the pouring rain.

He couldn't contain his excitement. "It's not a cave." he cried, fighting his way through a rain soaked bush. "We're back on course. It's the entrance to an old tunnel!"

13

Into the Hillside

"This is amazing," said Alf, his voice echoing into the eerie blackness beyond. "Even the track itself is still here. Look!" He pointed at the huge wooden sleepers. The twins stepped into the tunnel.

The more they walked, the darker and more uninviting their surroundings became. A strange smell hung in the air and strands of sooty black cobwebs brushed against their faces as they ventured into the unknown.

"Let's come back tomorrow when it's brighter," suggested Chrissy.

"We may never find our way back here," said Alf. He wanted to go on exploring. He felt as though the track itself was drawing him in deeper and deeper. There was no turning back now.

Chrissy walked back to the mouth of the tunnel to see if it was still raining. She sat on one of the sleepers and watched the water pouring through the trees. Alf plunged even farther into the hillside, thinking about the storm that had destroyed part of Thurhorn Bridge all those years before.

Alf found alcoves at regular intervals along the walls. He guessed that these must have been spaces that workmen stood in when they heard a train coming. Alf stepped into one of the alcoves and imagined what it must have been like with a steam locomotive thundering by.

His eyes were attracted by a glint of metal on the ground. Brushing cobwebs from his face, he bent down to investigate. It was a silver whistle on a long chain.

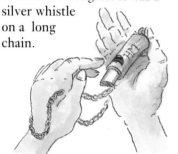

Alf ran back to the tunnel entrance so that he could show Chrissy what he'd found. "I think it's made of silver," he said. "I expect it's quite old. It must have been used by a guard when trains still ran through here."

Chrissy studied the whistle and chain carefully. "It can't have been lying in here for very long," she said. "Look how bright and shiny it is. Silver turns all black after a time if you don't keep polishing it . . ."

A sudden hissing made Chrissy bite her tongue. Alf jumped with fright at the noise. Dreading what they might see, they slowly turned to look back into the yawning depths of the tunnel.

At first, they saw nothing. Then, out of nowhere, something was hurtling toward them at great speed. Two glowing yellow circles hung in the darkness, growing bigger and bigger as they got rapidly nearer. They couldn't be . . . it wasn't possible . . . Were these the lights of an oncoming train? The twins ran in blind panic.

15

The Chase

Chrissy and Alf spilled out into the daylight and the lashing rain, convinced that they were about to be confronted by some unearthly train.

Out in the open, they stopped to catch their breath. All the twins could hear was the sound of their own blood pumping through their veins. No hissing of steam. No ghostly wails. Cautiously, they made their way back to the tunnel entrance.

Their relief soon turned to a different kind of horror as a beast launched itself out of the darkness. It was just recognizable as a cat, but it wasn't like any other cat, or any other animal, either of them had ever seen. It was huge, with bald patches in its fur and it only had one ear. But what was really strange about this beast was its eyes. Glowing brighter than hot coals in a fire, they had no pupils. It snarled at the twins, curling back its gums to reveal a set of yellowing fangs, as it hurtled through the air toward Alf.

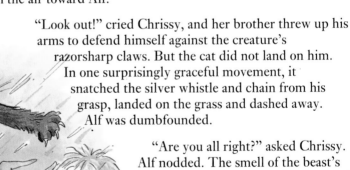

"Look out!" cried Chrissy, and her brother threw up his arms to defend himself against the creature's razorsharp claws. But the cat did not land on him. In one surprisingly graceful movement, it snatched the silver whistle and chain from his grasp, landed on the grass and dashed away. Alf was dumbfounded.

"Are you all right?" asked Chrissy. Alf nodded. The smell of the beast's breath still filled his nostrils. Beads of sweat had formed on his forehead.

The creature appeared in the nearby undergrowth, the whistle and chain hanging tantalizingly between its jaws. "We must get the whistle back," Alf shouted. "It could be important." Without even stopping to consider what they would do if they managed to catch the beast, the twins set off in hot pursuit.

16

They chased the cat for what seemed like miles. Sometimes they would lose sight of it and then its head would suddenly appear from behind a tree or pop up by a rock right next to them. It was almost as if the cat was playing with them, speeding ahead to make them follow then slowing down to let them keep up.

"I give up," said Alf at last, clutching his side and trying to catch his breath. He collapsed on a patch of wet grass. Looking across at Chrissy, he realized that it had stopped raining. Then he

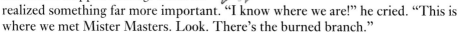

realized something far more important. "I know where we are!" he cried. "This is where we met Mister Masters. Look. There's the burned branch."

"You're right," laughed Chrissy. "The cat thought it was leading us around in circles, but it's almost led us home. The station isn't far from here."

When they reached the old station and climbed the steps to the platform, they were in for yet another surprise. Just outside the front doors lay the whistle and chain.

Chrissy looked down at the whistle and chain. Both were battered and the silver was tarnished with dull grey patches. "It's the same whistle for sure. It has the letters engraved on it, but it looks so much older. This is crazy!"

17

A Link with the Past

Uncle Jack was very excited when they showed him the whistle. He claimed that he was only interested in it as a piece of local history, but both Alf and Chrissy could tell that it meant more to him than that. There was a strange look in his eyes, and he wanted to know exactly where they had found it. He made the twins feel uneasy.

He went over to a shelf and pulled out an old photo album. He blew dust off it and flipped through the pages. "There," he said pointing to a black and white photograph of a man in a guard's uniform. He had a small flag in one hand and a whistle on a chain in the other. "In those days, all the guards would have had whistles like the one you found." Alf and Chrissy studied the old picture with interest. Their whistle certainly looked similar to the one in the guard's hand.

Uncle Jack handed Chrissy the whistle and she hung it around her neck on the chain. "You should show it to Mister Masters when you see him tomorrow morning," he said, and put the album back on the shelf. "You didn't find anything else did you?" he asked. "Or see anything? Nothing odd? No strange noises?" The twins felt awkward at this sudden stream of questions. They said nothing.

Uncle Jack frowned. "Is there something you're not telling me?" he demanded. There was a sense of urgency in his voice.

The twins looked at each other. They weren't going to tell him about the enormous cat with the glowing eyes . . . "Of course not," said Chrissy.

"Nothing out of the ordinary," Alf added. "Can we eat soon? I'm starving."

After a supper of three boiled eggs each, the twins went straight to their bedroom. Once they were inside the old Left Luggage Office, however, they didn't go to bed. They discussed the day's events in low whispers.

"I keep feeling the need to do things without quite knowing why," whispered Alf . "When we were in the tunnel I felt like a piece of metal being drawn to a huge magnet . Do you know what I mean?"

His sister nodded. "It's all somehow connected to the old Seabry-to-Thurhorn line. I know it is," said Chrissy. "And I bet Uncle Jack knows much more than he's letting on."

Chrissy was right. Little did they know that their uncle was lurking outside the door to the Left Luggage Office at that very moment. He stood very still, trying not to make a sound, straining to hear what they had to say about the day's events.

I must keep an even closer eye on those two from now on, he thought. I must be careful, very careful, or things could get out of hand.

Things of Interest

The next morning, Alf and Chrissy went to the home of Harold Masters. It was a tumbled down cottage at the edge of the village. Chrissy found a note pinned to the front door of the cottage. It read: TWINS. HAVE HAD TO GO OUT ON URGENT BUSINESS. PLEASE GO INSIDE. YOU WILL FIND SOME THINGS OF INTEREST ON THE TABLE. It was signed 'Harold Masters'.

Chrissy pushed open the door nervously. At first, they couldn't find the 'things of interest'. The only things on the table were old newspaper clippings. Then Chrissy noticed just how old the clippings were.

THURHORN BRIDGE DISASTER
Train crashes. No survivors.

In one of the worst storms this century, the river Thur burst its banks on Tuesday and washed away part of the Thurhorn Bridge viaduct. The bridge carries the line between the village of Seabry and Thurhorn. The 7:15pm train from Seabry, pulled by the steam locomotive *The Gypsy Bell*, is thought to have plummeted two hundred feet from the bridge into the river below. The Gravel Hill Rail Company say that there were thirty passengers and six crew members on board.

Sergeant Able Morris.

Sergeant Able Morris, who was in charge of the search party, told reporters: 'There is no sign of the train or its passengers or crew. The rain was so heavy and fell so quickly that the river Thur rose over ten feet in a matter of hours. I am sad to report that there is no hope of anyone having survived such a tragedy. I have never been interviewed by reporters before and would like to say hello to my mother and anyone else who reads what I have said.'

Thurhorn-to-Seabry line, famous for its many bends.

Masters Family t sell Briary Manor

Jonathan Masters is to sell Briar Manor which has belonged to his family for over 200 years. Mr. Masters's lawyer, Mr. Ben Horace, said that it was with great regret that the manor was being put up for sale.

"Since the loss of his son William in the Thurhorn Bridge Disaster, Mr. Masters wishes to start a new life with his wife and remaining son, Harold, away from Seabry."

Identical twins Harold and William were a familiar sight to ocal residents.

Briary Manor

"I have no doubt that the whole family will be sorely missed," said Mr. Horace.

"Look," she said. "These are over eighty years old. They're reports on the Seabry-to-Thurhorn line and the night of the storm."

"And if you're right about all the weird goings-on being connected to the old station and track . . . " began Alf.

"Exactly," his sister interrupted. "Then these old newspaper reports might give us some vital clues." They spread the clippings out on the table and read through them.

Famous Mystic Missing

The world famous mystic Marcus Hillcutty is thought to have been on the ill-fated train journey across the Thurhorn Bridge.

Marcus Hillcutty, who has performed mystical feats for presidents, royalty and anyone else with enough money to pay him, was going to Thurhorn for the annual meeting of The Society For Men With Impressive Beards of which he was President. He never arrived.

Marcus Hillcutty is probably most famous for making the fabulous Akimbo diamond disappear during a performance at the court of King Gulash of Gaberdeen. Unfortunately, he was unable to make it reappear, claiming that 'he was not as good at that part'. He narrowly avoided a prison sentence.

This year's meeting of The Society For Men With Impressive Beards has been cancelled out of respect for the missing mystic.

World famous Mar...

SEABRY-TO-THURHORN LINE TO CLOSE

Following the recent Thurhorn Bridge disaster, the President of the Gravel Hill Rail Company has announced that the Seabry-to-Thurhorn line is to close.

'This is out of respect for those involved in the accident,' Sir Nigel Lyer said. 'It is not because we cannot afford to repair the bridge. Honestly.'

'GYPSY BELL' DRIVER WAS LOCAL MAN

The driver of the steam locomotive The Gypsy Bell which was pulling the 7:15 from Seabry was Samuel 'Safety' Stevens. He had lived in Seabry all his life and, until the accident, had the best safety record of all the drivers working for the Gravel Hill Rail Company.

'If anyone broke so much as a fingernail on one of his trains it was unusual,' said a company spokesman. 'If there was any way to save his passengers on that bridge, Mister 'Safety' Stevens would have done it. He was a professional and popular man.'

With him on the footplate was fireman Wally Walters whose job it was to stoke the boiler. The guard was Henry Moose another popular Seabry inhabitant. Moose's mother, Amanda Moose (64) is well known locally for her work with sick seagulls.

A sick seagull.

The Village of Lost Hope

The twins were puzzled by the newspaper clippings. They were about the Thurhorn Bridge disaster and nothing else. Surely Harold Masters had more to tell them than that? Alf and Chrissy felt none the wiser, and decided that the village itself might hold some clue.

Seabry turned out to be a sad place. A sense of gloom hung in the air. Time had been cruel to the village. What were once pretty houses and cottages were now neglected and decayed. Windows were broken, plaster was cracked and tiles were falling off roofs. In the middle of the village stood a monument with a statue of a steam locomotive on top. The twins went to take a closer look.

It's as if nobody cares about this place.

It's so dull and lifeless.

An inscription was carved into the old and crumbling stone, which read: IN MEMORY OF THE VICTIMS OF THE THURHORN BRIDGE DISASTER. When Alf walked around the monument, he discovered something else was written on the other side. He couldn't read it because it was covered with moss. "Did you bring your pocketknife?" he asked Chrissy.

Chrissy took a knife from her pocket and they began to scrape away the moss. Alf used his fingers. Soon they had uncovered the words: 'PLEASE HELP US'. The twins wondered what it could mean.

Alf looked at the gloomy, unloved houses surrounding the green. Fences were broken and rotting, and weeds grew through cracks in the paths. Even the ducks in the muddy village pond looked depressed. He decided that the place could certainly do with some help.

Chrissy interrupted his thoughts with a cry. "Look!" she said, pointing with a shaking hand at a second row of moss covered letters. They seemed to shimmer into place before their very eyes. "T-T-Those weren't there a moment ago!" Goose pimples rose on the twins' flesh and they felt icily cold.

Alf and Chrissy frantically set about scraping off the moss. Because the words were so familiar to them, they both knew what the letters spelled before they'd even cleaned them all. It was their own names.

Were they dreaming? Had they gone mad? The letters weren't freshly carved. They had been worn by the weather, and by time itself . . . but these were their names, and it was no coincidence. It was as if this was a desperate plea for help reaching out to them across the years.

Chrissy's head began to spin. She put her hand out to steady herself, and touched the statue of *The Gypsy Bell*. Her arm tingled violently, and everything around them became a whirling blur of sight and sounds.

Suddenly, Alf and Chrissy were plunged into total darkness and felt a gust of wind against their faces. There was the deafening screech of metal on metal. The air became thick with choking smoke, and light appeared out of nowhere. "Look out!" screamed Alf.

A Nightmare Journey

They were back in the tunnel! Alf grabbed Chrissy by the arm and pulled her into one of the alcoves, pressing himself flat against the cold slimy wall. A split second later, a steam train came screeching out of the empty darkness and thundered by, shaking the ground beneath them.

This was no ordinary train. It glowed like white-hot metal and was driven by a man with a crazed look in his eyes. Next to him on the footplate stood a second man, blackened with soot, frantically stoking the boiler with a shovel.

Grey and desperate faces seemed to stare from every window, eyes wide and helpless. A ghostlike child had his hands pressed against the glass.

As the locomotive reached the tunnel opening and daylight, it dissolved into nothing. Each of the four coaches in turn did the same. When the last coach disappeared, there was a deafening silence . . .

Tales to Tell

"Are you all right?" asked a familiar voice. Alf sat up, his head still spinning. He rubbed his eyes and looked into the concerned face of Harold Masters. They were on the village green.

"What have you two been up to?" asked the old man. "You're covered in soot." Alf and Chrissy looked at their clothes. He was right.

The twins were at a loss for words. They felt as though they had just woken from a deep sleep which they couldn't quite shake off. Standing up, the ground felt shaky underfoot and their minds felt scrambled.

Mister Masters insisted that they come back to his cottage. While Alf had a bath and Chrissy a shower, the old man proudly produced some clean clothes for them to wear. Later they all sat together in his huge red chairs.

Feeling clean but confused, Alf and Chrissy told the old man about the carved message asking them for help by name, and about the train. "It was a ghost train . . . It was there but, at the same time, it wasn't . . ." Chrissy finished.

"You probably think we're crazy," said Alf.

Harold Masters shook his head and smiled. "You couldn't be more wrong," he said. "What you've told me is exactly what I've been hoping to hear. For over eighty years most people in Seabry have thought *I* was crazy, but what you've just said changes everything. Let me explain . . ."

Alf and Chrissy had never really thought about there being a special bond between twins before. But what about those birthdays when they had bought each other exactly the same presents? Maybe that explained it. There could be some invisible force that linked one twin to another.

"But what we saw was a *ghost* train, Mister Masters," said Alf. "Doesn't that prove that your brother is . . . a ghost?"

"The writing on the monument was a plea for help," said Harold Masters with a faraway look. "And those able to ask for help are able to be saved!"

27

Revelations

I t was early evening when the twins left Harold Masters's cottage, their soot-covered clothes in a bag. They walked back toward the station, going over what the old man had told them.

"How can Mister Masters believe that his brother Bill is still out here somewhere?" asked Chrissy. "It doesn't make sense. Bill Masters was on that train when it crashed years ago, and now we've actually seen a train full of ghosts. What more proof does he want?"

Alf's eyes lit up. "That's it. Proof!" he cried. "What proof do we have that the train went over the end of Thurhorn Bridge in the storm? Think about it. According to Mister Masters and the newspaper clippings, nobody actually saw it go into the river and no wreck was ever found. Maybe it never happened!"

Chrissy frowned. "If it didn't go over the bridge, where did the train disappear to on the night of the storm? And if there wasn't an accident, why did we run into a train full of ghosts this afternoon?" Alf's idea seemed ridiculous but, at the same time, there was something about it that made a strange kind of sense.

"Oh well," sighed Alf. "It was just a thought." They arrived back at the station and went inside. Uncle Jack looked up from a large book he was reading.

"Hello," he smiled. "Perfect timing. Supper's ready."

Meow.

How did you get in here?

The nightmare journey to the tunnel and back had left the twins exhausted. After supper, they were asleep within minutes of going to bed . . . then came the voices. Chrissy thought she was imagining things, until she saw Alf was also sitting up and listening. A chorus of desperate whispering filled the room. Words were spoken quickly and frantically until, quite suddenly, they fell silent and the twins remembered nothing else until morning.

They woke up bursting with energy. The sun was shining, Salmon was purring, and their heads were filled with new ideas and understanding. Now they somehow knew that they had been *chosen* to see and hear certain things. Had the whispering voices told them? Without speaking, both Alf and Chrissy hurried over to the window and looked out into the woods.

"The noise we've heard wasn't the hooting of an owl, but the tooting of the steam whistle on the ghost train," said Chrissy, looking past the crack in the glass to the trees beyond.

" I know," Alf nodded. "But some things still need explaining. I mean, what does this cracked window have to do with a ghost train? Maybe it did just crack in the heat."

Chrissy stared at the crack and her eyes opened wide with excitement. "No, don't you see?" she cried. "Don't you see?"

Don't you see?

The Trek Through the Woods

Chrissy pointed at the crack. "It's a kind of map!" she said. "Perhaps there's a special place you need to stand for it to work. You try. Stand here." She stepped aside and Alf took her place. He was stunned. From the parts of the woods he could recognize, the crack lined up with the route of the old track. What mysterious force could create a crack in glass in such a precise pattern?

It's more of a picture than a map.

"I wonder if it's an instruction," Chrissy suggested. "It could be telling us to follow the old track. We turned back at the tunnel last time." Her heart was beating faster with excitement. Somehow she *knew* that she was right. Alf felt it too.

Just then, a large moth landed on the window, near the top of the crack in the glass. Chrissy tried to shoo it away with her hand. "No. Wait," said Alf. "If the crack is some kind of map, what does this moth look like?"

"Some weird kind of insect," said Chrissy, wondering what her brother was getting at.

"No. It looks like an X," said Alf. He could see a rock sticking up through the trees, past the moth. "We've got to go to this spot."

"We'll never find it," said Chrissy. "Don't forget how overgrown parts of the track are. And this isn't an ordinary map. We can't take it with us."

"We'll find a way, I'm sure of it," said Alf. "Let's go."

X marks the spot.

Uncle Jack was nowhere to be seen, so they grabbed what they needed without having to explain. They borrowed two old fashioned lanterns, in case they went back inside the tunnel, and hastily filled their backpacks, before dashing off into the woods. "Do you think we'll see the ghost train again?" asked Alf, with a slight tremor in his voice. Chrissy raised her eyebrows and shrugged her shoulders. Who knew what lay ahead of them . . . ?

They passed the blackened branch in the clearing where they'd first met Harold Masters, and walked deeper and deeper into the woods. Just when it became impossible to find the remains of the old track, there was a scrambling and rustling noise from the undergrowth. The beast with the glowing eyes came out from behind a bush and leaped onto a branch in front of them. It faced them with its blank expression but somehow seemed smaller, and far less threatening than before.

I think we're supposed to follow it.

Friend or foe?

The beast stood up and began to walk away, quickly followed by Alf and Chrissy who were afraid they might lose sight of it. They began to trust their guide, but this didn't stop them feeling nervous when they reached the yawning entrance to the tunnel. Gingerly, they stepped inside. No ghostly train appeared as they made their way through the blackness. They came out the other end unshaken, but blinking in the sunlight. Moments later, they were led to a clearing with a large outcrop of rock in the middle. They had reached the spot. What now?

H-Help!

Exhausted, Alf sat down and slipped off his backpack. "We're here," he said and turned just in time to see Chrissy being swallowed up by the ground. She let out a piercing scream.

Exploring Below

Chrissy blinked and tried to get used to the darkness. Where was she? What had happened? There was a small circle of light way above her, but that was all. She fumbled in her backpack and pulled out one of the lanterns and a box of matches. The match spluttered to life and the lantern flickered then gave off a red glow.

Holding the lantern high, Chrissy inspected her new surroundings. She had fallen into an underground cave of some sort, with the roof and walls supported by massive wooden props. Shadowy passages led off in all directions. The air smelled dank and musty. She shuddered.

"CHRISSEEEEE!" echoed a voice from above. Alf's face appeared through the hole in the roof. "Are you okay?" he called. His eyes hadn't had time to adjust to the dark, so all he could see was a red glow.

"Fine! A little bruised, that's all." Chrissy shouted. "Get the rope, and come on down."

Alf took the rope from his backpack and tied one end to a tree. He lowered the other end down the hole and climbed slowly into the gloom.

When he reached the bottom, Chrissy gave him the matches. Soon his lantern was giving off a green glow. He looked around in wide eyed amazement. "These tunnels could stretch for miles," he gasped.

Something clicked in Chrissy's brain. "We're in an old mine! There was one on the map in the newspaper clippings."

32

We can find our way back by following the arrows.

Alf took a piece of chalk from his pocket and drew arrows along the wall at regular intervals. "I hope we don't meet any ghosts down here," he said after a while. He tried to make it sound like a joke.

"If this was where X marked the spot and where the cat meant to lead us, maybe we're supposed to come face-to-face with some ghosts about now," Chrissy suggested. She looked out for the strange beast's glowing eyes somewhere in the darkness.

The deeper into the mine they went, the more stale the air and the more eerie their surroundings became. They reached the end of the tunnel and found themselves in a vast cavern. Both of the twins had the unsettling feeling that they were being watched. Alf felt a lump in his throat as he held up his green lantern to illuminate the velvet blackness. A thousand eyes glinted back at them.

W-W-We're not alone.

33

Rockfall

"They're only bats," said Chrissy, squinting into the inky darkness. "Nothing to worry about. They're probably more frightened of us than we are of them."

"Who said I was worried?" said Alf.

"You look a bit green, that's all," Chrissy grinned.

"It's the light," said Alf. "I just hope that they're ordinary bats." He eyed them nervously, thinking of the weird cat and the huge brown moth. "Let's keep moving."

The twins crossed the cavern and discovered the entrances to two tunnels hewn into the solid rock wall. They didn't have the cat to lead the way, and no mysterious voices whispered to them. They had to decide which one to take. They picked the tunnel on the left.

Chrissy went first, her red lantern casting eerie shadows on the underground

> Let's stick together. Which way shall we go?

> Let's try this one.

passageway. The air was hot and stale and there was a strange rumbling sound somewhere up ahead in the darkness. Oh no, thought Alf. It's the ghost train.

"There's no turning back now," Chrissy shouted above the noise.

Suddenly, the walls of the tunnel began to shake violently, and pieces of rock and soil fell from the roof. The twins felt the ground rumble beneath them. They did their best to steady themselves.

Out of the corner of his eye, Alf saw something move above him, "Watch out!" he warned as a chunk of rock the size of a melon smashed the lantern from his grasp.

A cloud of dust came swirling toward the twins and they coughed and spluttered in the confusion. "I can't breathe," Chrissy choked, holding her hand up to her face.

The cloud was caused by part of a wall collapsing farther up the tunnel. One of the enormous wooden props holding up the roof began to groan under the weight of the thousands of tons of earth and rock above it. It sounded like the unearthly moans of some dying giant.

I don't like the sound of this. Let's get out of here!

The groaning stopped when the prop snapped in half and fell to the ground with a deafening CRASH. A few feet ahead of the twins, the roof started to cave in. The earth seemed to shift beneath them and both Alf and Chrissy lost their balance and fell to the ground.

Chrissy scrambled to her feet. "We've got to go back!" she yelled. "This whole place is going to come down on us."

The twins turned and ran back the way they'd come, but it was too late. Their path was blocked off by a freshly-fallen pile of rocks. "We're trapped," cried Alf, as another cloud of dust billowed toward them.

Confession from a Mystic

"I knew we shouldn't have trusted that cat and followed it here," said Chrissy, rubbing her elbow which felt a bit bruised. The rumbling had stopped when the last rock had fallen, and now the dust was beginning to settle.

"This mine can't have been used for ages," said Alf. "We're going to have to try to dig our way out if there's no other way." They hadn't thought to pack a shovel in their backpacks. "Let's look around."

They had only been exploring for a minute or two when they made a discovery. The rockfall had opened up a hole in one of the walls, leading to the other tunnel. Alf climbed through it without a moment's hesitation, and immediately tripped over something. "Careful," warned Chrissy and hurried across with the lantern. She held it up to reveal her brother sprawled over a pile of . . . bones. It was a skeleton.

Alf leaped to his feet. The skeleton was wearing a few dusty rags that must once have been a man's clothes. In his bony hand was a book.

Alf gulped and pried the book from the skeleton's fingers. He opened it. Chrissy stood beside him, holding up the lantern casting a red light on the yellowing pages.

To Whomsoever Shall Find Me

This is an account of my actions on the night of Tuesday last and I, Marcus Hillcutty pray that I shall not solely be judged a bad man. My intentions were good.

Myself

1

As the most celebrated passenger aboard the 7:15 train to Thurhorn I was invited by the driver of the locomotive (a Mr Stevens) to stand with him upon the footplate of 'The Gypsy Bell'.

2

I was, therefore, with him when we began to cross the bridge over the river Thur and together we witnessed it collapsing before our very eyes. Using my mystic powers, learned after many years of study, I muttered an incantation to save the train and all on board from a terrible fate.

3

I sent the train to Limbo in a matter of seconds. It is not a place in the same way that Seabry is a place. Limbo is nowhere It is a place out of time. My plan was somehow to bring back the train when the danger of the storm and the broken bridge had passed.

4

Unfortunately, I fell from the speeding locomotive moments before it disappeared and I crawled, wounded, to the safety of this mine. I know that I shall not recover from my injuries, but it is the others I feel for.

5

I have condemned the passengers and crew to a fate worse than death. Oh, Now they must ride on an endless journey until the end of time itself. They never grow so much as a day older, but feel every second passing by on their neverending train ride to nowhere. Forgive

Alf turned the page once more. There was no writing on the next page. The rest of the book was blank.

The Search for Daylight

At last the twins understood why the mystic forces had wanted them to go to the abandoned mine ever since they had arrived in Seabry. If what Marcus Hillcutty had written in his notebook was true, and not the rantings of a dying man, the people on the ghost train were not ghosts at all. They were alive, but trapped out of time and in need of help. What didn't make sense to Alf and Chrissy was why *they* had been asked to help.

A sense of urgency suddenly swept over them. They had to get out of the mine fast. There was only one way to go, and that was to follow the tunnel that wasn't blocked off. After what seemed hours, they spotted daylight streaming through an opening, and a blast of fresh air smelling of . . . the sea! Alf and Chrissy scrambled up a pile of rocks and crawled through the gap onto a hillside.

Far below them stood Thurhorn Bridge, still bearing the scars of the storm of over eighty years before. Chrissy tried to imagine Marcus Hillcutty on the footplate of *The Gypsy Bell*, calling out an incantation in a desperate bid to save the train from steaming off the end . . . and condemning the passengers and crew to a timeless journey to nowhere.

Before either of them had time to fully take in their new surroundings, the twins' heads began to spin. Alf and Chrissy swayed dangerously from side to side. They were hundreds of feet up, which was why, way below, the River Thur looked like a harmless ribbon of blue.

"I think I'm going to fall!" screamed Alf.

"What's happening?" cried Chrissy. She shut her eyes tight to try to stop her head from spinning. When she opened them again, she found that she and Alf were no longer on the hillside.

Alf looked around in horror and amazement. "We're on the ghost train somewhere in Hillcutty's Limbo," he whispered in horror and amazement. "If what he wrote was true, we're out of time and place."

They stood in a compartment beside two men who sat playing a card game. Every inch of every wall seemed to be covered in pencil marks. Then the truth dawned on the twins. These men must have been playing cards for over eighty years, but probably looked as young as the day they stepped on board.

One of the players smiled triumphantly and laid down his cards. "I win," he said and leaned back to make a mark on the floor with a pencil. Then Alf and Chrissy realized the awful truth. Unless the twins could somehow help these men, and everyone on board this doomed train, they would go on playing cards until the end of time . . . and would still keep score.

In another compartment, there sat a young woman. Chrissy found it almost impossible to believe that she must have been born over eighty years before.

If she hadn't been on a train whisked out of natural time by Marcus Hillcutty's misuse of unearthly powers, what would the woman have looked like? Would her hair have grown down to her waist and turned white long ago? Here it was as short and brown as the day she climbed aboard. The woman turned toward the twins, but did not seen to notice them.

The Truth is Told

Suddenly the scene changed, and Alf and Chrissy found themselves standing by a boy with his back to them. He was staring out of a window.

"I know you can hear me, Harold," he said. "Please help us. Send us the Alf and Chrissy you think about. Perhaps they are our only hope . . ."

The twins knew at once who they were watching. It was Bill Masters, Harold's twin brother. It seemed hard to believe that the boy was really the same age as old Harold Masters.

Alf and Chrissy's heads spun once more, and they found that they had returned to the hillside. Perhaps they had never actually left it. They were lying in the grass with Uncle Jack standing over them. He looked worried.

"Are you hurt?" he asked, concerned. "I knew it would come to this." They followed their uncle down the hillside to where he'd parked his car. "You'd better tell me exactly what you've been up to," he added, as they climbed into the back seat.

The twins decided that it was time to share their secret with someone. Everything seemed to be getting out of control. Who knew where it might lead them next? They had to take a chance and trust their uncle. On the way back to his home, they told him what had happened since they'd arrived in Seabry.

40

Uncle Jack was a very good listener and didn't interrupt with a lot of stupid questions. By the time they returned to the station, they had finished their incredible story.

He walked through the front door and straight over to the bookshelf between the Left Luggage and Ticket offices. Above it hung a framed black and white photograph.

"You say that the big black cat you followed has only one ear?" he asked. The twins nodded. "Is this the one you saw?" He pointed to a cat in the photograph.

"That's it all right," said Alf. "But now it has amazing eyes ."

Their uncle took the photograph down from the wall and turned it over. "Read what it says on the back," he said. Alf and Chrissy read the words written in faded ink. "Arthur Bolt was Seabry's very last station master," he explained.

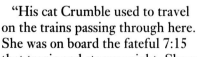

ARTHUR BOLT
and
CRUMBLE
(aged 10)

"His cat Crumble used to travel on the trains passing through here. She was on board the fateful 7:15 that tragic and stormy night. She must be over ninety years old now."

Alf suddenly realized what this meant. If Crumble had managed to returned from *The Gypsy Bell* in Limbo, then it might be possible for the people on board to do the same. "If only we could find a way to help the poor passengers and crew," he said.

"If anyone can, you two can," said Uncle Jack mysteriously. "I think it's time I told you something about yourselves." He began to tell a strange tale . . .

The Power Behind The Beards

A hundred years ago, a group of people set up 'The Society For Men With Impressive Beards', and met in Thurhorn once a year.

To the outside world, they seemed a bunch of fools.

In fact, the beards were just a front. These were some of the greatest minds of the day meeting in secret. Most of their beards were false. Some of the so-called bearded men were even women...

The president of the society was Marcus Hillcutty. Many people thought that his mystic magic was fake. We know that it was genuine.

The members of the society were working on a way to develop the power of the human mind...

Alf and Chrissy were dumbstruck. They didn't feel that they had any special powers!

"You have, but you haven't been shown how to use them yet," said Uncle Jack. "They're there, buried deep inside you. You've seen their effects already. It was your minds that made the window crack to show you the route of the old track . . . and made the moth appear just as you were wondering where you were supposed to go. What you have to do now is to learn to control this power to put right a wrong. Hillcutty misused his powers, even though he was trying to help. He broke the laws of Nature. By taking the ghost train out of time, he changed the natural order of things. In fact, he changed history. Your job will be to try to put things back as they should have been before Hillcutty interfered. If you can do that, you'll be creating a new beginning for us all. We'll all be living the lives we would have led if the mystic hadn't messed things up."

"Wow!" gasped Alf. "You mean we could change history?"

"No, that would be dangerous. It was Hillcutty who changed the course of history. You will be trying to put things back as they should be. You will not only be trying to put the ghost train back on the right rails, but also time itself," said Uncle Jack. "I have been watching you ever since you arrived, waiting for the right time to reveal these secrets to you. You are twins, and often share feelings and thoughts. The people on the train were able to tap into the combined power of your minds."

I too have some of the powers developed by your great-grandmother . . . but, as twins, yours are twice the strength.

43

Using the Power

Uncle Jack explained the power developed by 'The Society For Men With Impressive Beards' to the twins. This was the power of thought, which their great-grandmother had helped to control. There was no spoon bending or tomfoolery. Under his watchful eye, Alf and Chrissy very quickly learned how to use it.

Meow.

They began by sending messages to each other by concentrating very hard on them. Chrissy would say the words over and over again in her mind, and Alf would have to try to sense what she was thinking. After a while he could actually *feel* her thoughts in his head.

At one stage Salmon appeared to want to join in too. He kept on walking along the back of Chrissy's chair, rubbing against her shoulders. He only jumped down when Uncle Jack appeared with a bowl of boiled eggs.

After supper, Alf swapped roles with Chrissy. This time he did the thinking, and she had to picture what was in his mind.

I don't understand this one.

I'm saying it's time you changed your socks!

Before bed, their uncle congratulated them on their progress. "Tomorrow you must put the power to a very important use," he reminded them. "You must *think* the train into stopping." Salmon interrupted with a purr. "Once you have broken its endless journey, it should become a solid train once more, and enter real time at exactly the moment Marcus Hillcutty made it disappear all those years ago," Uncle Jack went on. "That means it won't go over the end of the bridge . . . But that's tomorrow's task. What you need now is a good night's sleep."

The next morning, all three of them were up early. The sun was still low in the sky and the grass wet with dew as they made their way through the woods. They reached the tunnel, took a deep breath and stepped into the gloom.

Now the twins had to try to summon the train simply by concentrating on it. There was a sudden screech of metal wheels on the track. The train thundered out of nowhere and steamed at breakneck speed toward Alf and Chrissy who stood their ground on the track. The driver frantically pulled on his steam whistle and it hooted its warning like some monstrous owl.

Alf and Chrissy didn't move. They tried to think the train into stopping and becoming a normal solid machine again. They had to return it to that stormy night over eighty years before, which was its rightful place in time. It was working! Seconds before it reached them, *The Gypsy Bell* became a solid object as they had planned . . . BUT IT DID NOT STOP.

The twins managed to leap into an alcove in the wall. They just missed being crushed under the solid pounding wheels of the steam train before it disappeared back in time to the dreadful storm.

"Oh no!" screamed Chrissy. "We've put history right, but killed them all! What sort of a new beginning is this?" Everything went black.

A New Beginning

Chrissy blinked. Alf blinked. They couldn't believe their eyes. They were no longer in the tunnel but were standing next to Uncle Jack in brilliant sunlight. He was lifting some luggage out of his car. "You'll like Seabry," he was saying. "There will be plenty to do while you're here."

In front of them was a house the twins had never seen before. Standing in the doorway was Harold Masters and another old man exactly like him. Alf and Chrissy couldn't tell them apart. "These are my friends Bill and Harold Masters," said their uncle. Then Alf and Chrissy understood . . . They had succeeded in changing history back to how it should have been!

Chrissy tried to remember what Uncle Jack had said would happen if they set time back on its rails. *"We'll all be living the lives we would have led if the mystic hadn't messed things up."* That was it. Everyone was now living in a new present . . . a present where they'd never met Harold Masters before! But how come Bill Masters was standing there, larger than life?

Alf was wondering the same thing. If they had sent the train back in time without stopping it, surely Bill Masters and all the other people on board must have hurtled off the end of the storm-wrecked bridge?

"We live over in Briary Manor," said Bill Masters, interrupting their thoughts. "We're having a party there on Sunday. Why not come over with your uncle? It's a double celebration."

"Yes," said Harold Masters. "Seabry has won the Best Kept Village Pond Competition again, and one of our local heroes is celebrating his one-hundred-and-tenth birthday. Here." He handed them a newspaper clipping. "This article from our local paper tells you all about him."

FREE BEARD TRIM AT MONICA'S

Simply bring this coupon to Monica's Salon and you're entitled to a thorough and professional beard trim free of charge.

This offer, to celebrate the salon's long association with The Society For Men With Impressive Beards, is only open to people with beards.

Haircuts are not offered as an alternative.

Alf and Chrissy read the clipping. They frowned and looked at each other. They reread the clipping. What did a free beard trim coupon have to do with saving lives? "I'm so sorry," said the old man. "I gave you the wrong clipping. Here's the one I meant you to read . . ."

'Safety Stevens' 110 this week

Samuel Stevens celebrates his 110th birthday this Friday. Better known as the engine driver Safety Stevens, he is famous for having saved the lives of all those on board the now infamous 7:15 to Thurhorn over eighty years ago.

When driving the train across Thurhorn Bridge in a terrible storm, he saw that part of the bridge had been washed away by the swollen river.

Unable to stop the train in time, he managed to disconnect his locomotive, *The Gypsy Bell*, from the rest of the train.

He, and those on board the footplate, then jumped clear.

The locomotive fell from the bridge into the raging waters below but the carriages stopped before reaching the edge.

Thanks to Safety Stevens's quick thinking, no one was killed and there was only one injury. Marcus Hillcutty, a famous mystic of the time, grazed his knee when jumping from the train. He had been riding alongside Safety Stevens on *The Gypsy Bell*.

That certainly explains why Bill Masters is alive and well, Alf thought when he had read the story. But why doesn't anyone else remember the other past?

"Probably because they don't have our combined powers," said Chrissy's voice inside his head.

Chrissy felt Salmon rubbing against her ankles. "That's funny," said Uncle Jack. "He's not usually that friendly with people he's never met before." Chrissy smiled to herself. Perhaps she and Alf weren't the only ones to remember their other past life after all . . . Perhaps Salmon also had some strange memory of the time when they had saved the ghost train to nowhere.

Did You Spot?

You can use this page to help spot things that could be useful in solving the mystery. First, there are hints and clues you can read as you go along. They will give you some idea what to look out for. Then there are extra notes to read which tell you more about what happened afterwards.

Hints and Clues

3 It isn't necessarily an owl. What else could it be?

4-5 Those ornaments and pictures are worth studying. And there may be more to that crack than at first meets the eye.

6-7 Smoke? Chrissy's theory isn't the only possibility.

8-9 Is someone - or something - watching them in the woods? Look closely.

10-11 Chrissy and Alf are twins and Harold Masters is also a twin. That's worth remembering.

12-13 Earthly train? Does Harold Masters know more than he's telling?

14-15 Take a close look at the whistle Alf has found.

16-17 A cat with one ear? Does it look at all familiar?

18-19 What's that by the plant on the shelf? A disguise? If so, what's it for? You may find out later.

20-21 It's important to study the names of the crew carefully. Something could fall into place. Seemingly silly things could turn out to be very important too.

22-23 You should know who the whistle belonged to by now, but don't jump to conclusions.

24-25 Can you name any of the people you can see aboard the train?

26-27 How did Harold Masters 'happen to be there' to find them? Was he just passing?

28-29 Things seem to be happening just when Chrissy and Alf want them to . . . Interesting.

30-31 Where can Chrissy have gone? What about checking the map in the newspaper clippings you saw earlier?

32-33 Not all those pairs of eyes are the same. It might be worth taking a closer look at the cavern . . .

34-35 Isn't that an old top hat in the shadows? Wasn't someone wearing one like that in an old photograph?

36-37 This notebook explains a great deal. Read it with care!

38-39 On board the train, the people and compartments seem solid not ghost like.

40-41 So Uncle Jack admits to having been watching the twins . . .

42-43 You should know who the fake beard on the bookcase belonged to by now.

44-45 Carefully examine the train going over the edge of the bridge.

46-47 This really is a new beginning, isn't it? It's as though Alf and Chrissy's adventure never happened.

In the End

Now that the past has been changed back to how it should have been did you notice these changes in the present?

. . . Uncle Jack doesn't live in Seabry Station. (In fact, the bridge was repaired and the trains still run from Seabry to Thurhorn.)

. . . Harold Masters lives in Briary Manor, the home he grew up in. His parents had no reason to sell the house and go abroad because they didn't lose Bill.

. . . Seabry isn't a village of lost hope. According to the local paper, it has won the Best Kept Village Pond Competition on more than one occasion.

. . . The Society For Men With Impressive Beards is still going strong. (Who knows, you might even have bumped into a member without knowing it.)

. . . Uncle Jack doesn't remember anything about the twins' adventure because his powers aren't as strong as theirs.

By the Way . . .

Did you spot:

. . . The silver whistle Alf found must have looked new as long as it was on the train. Once it was in 'real time' it began to age eighty years.

. . . The initials HM on the whistle stood for Henry Moose, the guard on the train (mentioned on page 21), not Harold Masters.

. . . Marcus Hillcutty had sent the Akimbo diamond into Limbo, and he couldn't get that back either!

. . . It was the twins' great-grandmother's fake beard on Uncle Jack's bookcase.

First published in 1993 by Usborne Publishing Ltd, Usborne House, 83-85 Saffron Hill, London EC1N 8RT, England. Copyright © 1993 Usborne Publishing Ltd.

The name Usborne and the device 🎈 are Trade Marks of Usborne Publishing Ltd.
Printed in the UK. U.E.

All rights reserved. No part of this publication may be reproduced, stored in a retrieval system, or transmitted in any form or by any means, electronic, mechanical, photocopying, recording or otherwise, without the prior permission of the publisher.

First published in America March 1994